Moose lived with his family
in a house in the woods.

Every evening after supper,
when they had all settled
comfortably around the fire
in their living room,
Moose would tell his family
a story.

Then, one evening, Moose couldn't think of a single story he hadn't told his family before.

"Why don't you *read* us a story," suggested Mrs Moose.

So Moose went to borrow a storybook from Bear next door.

But Bear didn't have a storybook.

Neither did any of the other animals who lived in the woods.

Not Badger. Not Fox.

Not Hare. Not Mole. Not the three Wild Pigs.

Not even the Beavers had a storybook that Moose could borrow.

So, next day, Moose went
to the Library in Town.

At the Library there were
lots and lots of storybooks
for Moose to borrow.

"How about *Little Red Riding Hood*?" suggested the Librarian.
"Or *Puss in Boots* or *Cinderella*?
You can borrow them all
if you like, Moose."

"My!" said Bear when she saw
all the storybooks.

And that evening, after supper, she brought her cubs along to hear Moose read *Little Red Riding Hood*.

Next day, Bear told Badger how exciting *Little Red Riding Hood* had been.

And, that evening, she came back to hear Moose read *Puss in Boots*. Only this time, as well as her cubs, Bear brought Badger with her, and Badger's Hubby and *their* cubs.

And the evening after that, as well as her cubs,
and Badger and Badger's Hubby and *their* cubs,
Bear brought Fox along to listen to *Cinderella.*
And Fox brought his Missus and *THEIR* cubs!

Hare came, too.
And Mole.

And the Wild Pigs brought
three litters of piglets.

"Come in! Come in!" said Moose.
"The more the merrier!"
But it was really rather a squash.

And poor Mrs Moose
was run off her feet
making cocoa
for everyone.

When the Beavers piled in,
it got so awfully crowded
in the Moose's living room
it was like being in a can
of sardines.

No-one could move!
Moose hardly had room
to read *Cinderella*.

And this was a pickle,
it really was.

COCOA
CINDERELLA

So, next morning,
Moose called the Librarian
on the telephone.

Then he went to the junkyard
and found an old bus.

24

And after he had fixed the bus up ...

and fitted it out ...

Moose drove it to the Library in Town.

The bus was loaded up with lots
and lots of storybooks ...

books for Bear to borrow, and for Badger,
and for all the other animals
who lived in the woods!

"But we can't read!"
said Bear.

So Moose taught Bear to read.

Then Bear taught Badger.

And Badger taught Fox.

Fox taught ... no, not Fox.
Mrs Moose taught Hare to read.

Then Hare
taught Mole.

Mole and Hare taught the three Wild Pigs.

And the Wild Pigs taught the Beavers.

Soon everyone was
borrowing storybooks
from the book bus ...

and taking them home
to read for themselves.

Or with their neighbours.

Because reading
together ...

is such good fun.

But no-one could read a story
like Moose could - and so
his living room still got full.

Only now it was just in a cosy way,
with never a whiff of sardines!

This book is dedicated to
Librarians everywhere.
*I.M.*

First published 2021 by Walker Books Ltd
87 Vauxhall Walk, London SE11 5HJ

This edition published 2022

10 9 8 7 6 5 4 3 2 1



This book has been typeset in Clarendon T

Printed in China



British Library Cataloguing in Publication Data:
a catalogue record for this book is available
from the British Library

ISBN 978-1-5295-0420-0

www.walker.co.uk

For Mike and Alia who created Ya Beach. ~ R. S.

For the inner child in us all, let your imagination run free! ~ Z. W.

First published in paperback by HarperCollins *Children's Books* in 2023

HarperCollins *Children's Books* is a division of HarperCollins*Publishers* Ltd
1 London Bridge Street, London SE1 9GF

www.harpercollins.co.uk

HarperCollins*Publishers*
Macken House, 39/40 Mayor Street Upper, Dublin 1, D01 C9W8, Ireland

1 3 5 7 9 10 8 6 4 2



ISBN: 978-0-00-847071-5

Rebecca Smith and Zoe Waring assert the moral right to be identified as the author and illustrator of the work respectively. A CIP catalogue record for this book is available from the British Library.

Printed and bound in Italy by Rotolito